LIONEL
◆ AND ◆
HIS FRIENDS

LIONEL

◆ AND ◆
HIS FRIENDS

by Stephen Krensky
pictures by Susanna Natti

PUFFIN BOOKS

For all the friends on Eaton Road
S.K.

For Michael Willsky
S.N.

PUFFIN BOOKS
Published by the Penguin Group
Penguin Putnam Books for Young Readers, 345 Hudson Street, New York, New York 10014, U.S.A.
Penguin Books Ltd, 27 Wrights Lane, London W8 5TZ, England
Penguin Books Australia Ltd, Ringwood, Victoria, Australia
Penguin Books Canada Ltd, 10 Alcorn Avenue, Toronto, Ontario, Canada M4V 3B2
Penguin Books (N.Z.) Ltd, 182-190 Wairau Road, Auckland 10, New Zealand

Penguin Books Ltd, Registered Offices: Harmondsworth, Middlesex, England

First published in the United States of America by Dial Books for Young Readers,
a division of Penguin Books USA Inc., 1996
Published in a Puffin Easy-to-Read edition by Puffin Books,
a member of Penguin Putnam Books for Young Readers, 1999

1 3 5 7 9 10 8 6 4 2

Text copyright © Stephen Krensky, 1996
Illustrations copyright © Susanna Natti, 1996
All rights reserved

THE LIBRARY OF CONGRESS HAS CATALOGED THE DIAL EDITION AS FOLLOWS:
Krensky, Stephen.
Lionel and his friends / by Stephen Krensky;
pictures by Susanna Natti.
p. cm.
Summary: Lionel and his friends have dinner, trade sandwiches at school, eavesdrop on Louise and
Emily, and play baseball.
ISBN 0-8037-1750-4 (trade). — ISBN 0-8037-1751-2 (library)
[1. Friendship—Fiction.] I. Natti, Susanna, ill. II. Title.
PZ7.K883Lh 1996 [Fic]—dc20 94-37434 CIP AC

Puffin Books ISBN 0-14-038742-0
Puffin® and Easy-to-Read® are registered trademarks of Penguin Books USA Inc.

Printed in Hong Kong

Reading Level 1.9

CONTENTS

THE IMPOSTOR

Lionel and his friend Max
were playing together at Lionel's house.
They went to the kitchen for a snack.
Lionel's mother was there,
putting away some groceries.
"Do you need any help?" Max asked.
"Thank you, Max," she said.
She looked at Lionel.
"You can help too," she said.

Lionel frowned.

As they were finishing,
Louise came home
wearing new sneakers.
"What do you think?"
she asked her mother.
"Perfect," said Mother.

"I like them too," said Max.

"You do?" said Louise.

She looked at Lionel.

"You could learn a few things
from your friends," she said.

Lionel frowned again.

At dinner Lionel's father asked Max

if he wanted more squash.

"Thanks," said Max.

"It's delicious."

Lionel frowned his biggest frown yet.

After dinner

Lionel pulled Max into his room.

"All right," he said, "what's going on?"

"What do you mean?" Max asked.

Lionel folded his arms.

"The real Max isn't so polite
and helpful," he said.

"He doesn't like new sneakers.
And he hates squash."

Lionel looked hard at Max.

"You're not the real Max.

You must be an impostor."

Max laughed.

"I am too the real Max," he said.

"Honest."

Lionel was not convinced.

"Who got in trouble last week
for flying paper airplanes in class?"

"Jeffrey," said Max.

"True," Lionel admitted.

"Now tell me Polly's middle name."

Max sighed.

"She doesn't have one," he said.

Lionel sighed.

"I guess you're the real Max,"

he said.

"Why are you acting so strange?"

"I don't know," said Max.

"But you acted the same way
at my house yesterday."

"I did?" said Lionel.

Max nodded.

"You offered to help my father
clean the basement," he said.
"And later you told my sister
how good her homework looked."
Lionel turned red.
"You're right."

"Maybe it's a disease,"
said Max.
"The kind you only catch
at other people's houses."

"Maybe," said Lionel.

"If it is, let's hope

we both get better soon."

THE SANDWICH

Lionel sat down

in the school cafeteria.

Everyone else started eating lunch.

Lionel just took out his sandwich

and put it on the table.

He stared at it.

"What's the matter, Lionel?"

asked Susie. "Why aren't you eating?"

Lionel sighed.

"My father made the wrong thing today," he said.

Jeffrey took a look.

"It's peanut butter and jelly," he said.

"That's what you always have."

Lionel shook his head.

"This is jelly and peanut butter,"
he said.

"My father made it wrong."

"He put the jelly on first."

Ellen nodded.

"Sometimes my mother

makes me chocolate milk.

She puts the milk in the glass

before the powder

instead of the other way around.

It never tastes the same."

"Why didn't your father make you

another sandwich?" Jeffrey asked.

Lionel frowned.

"He said there wasn't time."

"Maybe you could turn it over,"

said Susie.

Lionel shook his head.

"That wouldn't help," he said.

"Then it would just be

jelly and peanut butter upside down."

"You know, Lionel," said Neil,

"I like jelly and peanut butter

sandwiches.

Do you want to trade?"

Lionel's face brightened.

"What do you have instead?" he asked.

"Tuna fish," said Neil.

"Solid white?" Lionel asked.

Neil nodded.

"Cut in half sideways, not triangles?"

Neil nodded again.

"White bread?"

Neil nodded some more.

"Okay," said Lionel.

They made the trade.

Lionel inspected his new sandwich.

"By the way," he said,

"what kind of mayonnaise is this?"

"Regular," said Neil.

Good thing, thought Lionel,

as he happily took a bite.

THE MEETING

Lionel and Jeffrey were
crawling through the grass.
"Quiet," whispered Lionel.
"We're getting close.
And aliens have big ears."
Jeffrey lowered his head.
"Do you think they're dangerous?"
he asked.
Lionel thought so.

"After spending all that time in space,"
he said, "they're bound to be cranky.
Especially the ugly one
with the yellow hair."
They crept a little closer.

The alien with the yellow hair
was speaking.

"The time has come," said Louise.

"Are you sure?" said Emily.

"I'm sure," said Louise.

"I'm going to get rid of *him*
once and for all.
When I'm done,
there won't be a trace of *him* left."
Lionel and Jeffrey looked at each other.

What were these aliens plotting?

And who was this mysterious *him*

they were talking about?

They wriggled forward to hear more.

"How are you going to do it?"

asked Megan.

"I'm not sure," said Louise.

"There are so many possibilities."

"What about tying *him* to a rocket,"

said Emily,

"and blasting him into space?"

"Too uncertain," said Louise.

"He might come back,

like a comet or something."

"What about boiling *him* in oil?"

"Too messy," said Louise.

"I'd have to clean the pot afterward."

"Maybe quicksand," said Megan.

"Maybe," said Louise.

"It certainly would be neat."

"Won't your parents get suspicious?"

wondered Emily.

Louise shook her head.

"They'll believe whatever I tell them.

With Lionel anything's possible."

Lionel and Jeffrey shared

a horrified glance.

Lionel was the *him* they were discussing.

"Of course," said Emily,
"you still need to get your hands
on *him*."

Louise stood up to stretch.

"Oh, that won't be too hard. . . . "

She jumped over to where the boys were hiding.

"WILL IT, LIONEL?"

Both boys jumped up.

"Run!" cried Lionel.

"Run for your life!" said Jeffrey.

The three girls watched them go.

Then they started laughing.

"Did you see their faces?" said Emily.

"They'll think twice before sneaking up on us again," said Megan.

Louise sighed.

"At least for today," she said.

PLAY BALL

Lionel and his friends
were playing baseball.
Lionel was getting a lot of advice.
"Dive for those balls, Lionel,"
said Jeffrey, when a ball got past him.
"Catch with two hands," said Sarah,
when a ball jumped off his glove.
When Lionel came up to bat,
Ellen was pitching.
"Easy out," she said.

Lionel gripped the bat firmly.

He would show her how wrong she was.

Ellen made her windup.

The pitch sailed in.

Lionel waited—and then he swung hard.

The bat met the ball

with a sharp *Craaccck!*

The ball went up and up and up.

It sailed over a fence.

CRASH!

"That sounded like a window,"

said Max.

"At the Barries'," said Sarah.

Lionel froze.

He squeezed his eyes shut.

This was going to be terrible.

Mr. Barrie was bound to yell at him.

His parents would find out.

They would yell too.

Lionel opened his eyes.

Mr. Barrie was approaching

with a ball in his hand.

"Who hit this ball?" he asked.

Lionel swallowed hard.

He didn't want anyone else

getting in trouble for his mistake.

"I did," he said.

"I hit it too," said Jeffrey behind him.

He had picked up his bat.

"And me," said Max,

his bat now resting on his shoulder.

"I got a piece of it," said George.

"Don't forget me," said Sarah.

"And us," said everyone else together.

They were all holding their bats.

Mr. Barrie looked around.

"I see," he said, trying to look serious.

"It was a real team effort."

He rubbed his chin.

"Well, since you all shared in the hit,

you can all help me fix

the window later.

Fair enough?"

Everyone nodded.

Mr. Barrie returned to his house.

Lionel looked at everybody and sighed.

"Thanks," he said.

Jeffrey smiled.

"It could have been any of us.

Besides," he added,

"that's what friends are for."